DO NOT TOUCH ME THERE!

BY: KACY C. CHAMBERS

This book is dedicated to my son Carter, daughter Carsyn, and niece Loryn.

Girls and boys both have private parts.

You have private parts in the front and private parts in the back.

Front

Back

Private parts should be

private.

This means you should

NOT let anyone see

them or touch them.

PRIVATE
PROPERTY

There are only two reasons for anyone to ever touch or look at your private parts.

Reason #1:

Parents might need to wash your private parts for you when you are a baby.

When you become a big kid you can wash these body parts by yourself.

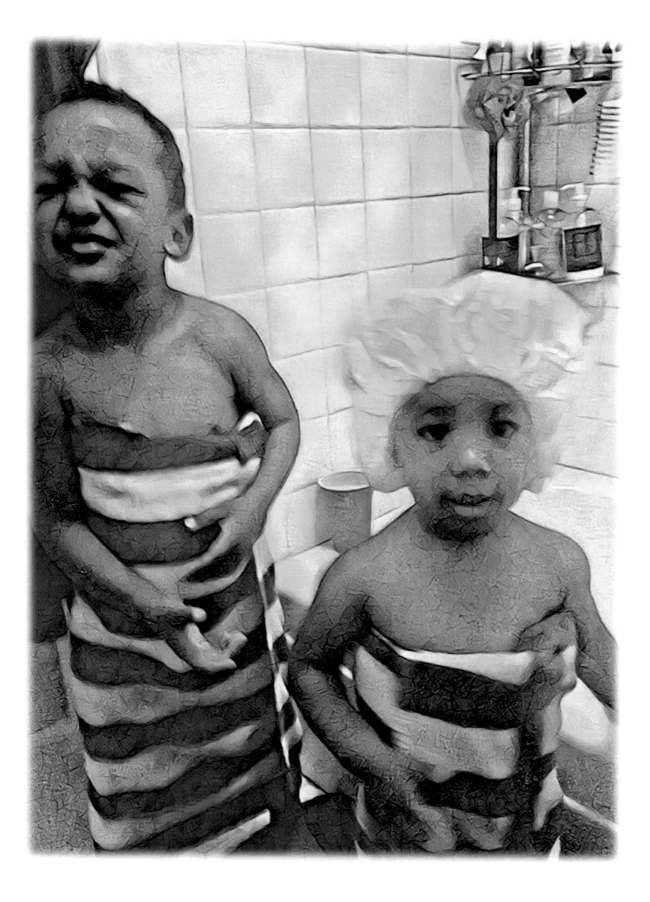

Reason #2:

Sometimes the doctor might have to examine your private parts.

Doctors should only do this while you are in the room with your parents.

Can my friends see them? **NO**

Can my uncle or aunt see them? **NO**

Can my sister or brother see them? **NO**

Can my cousin see them? **NO**

Can my teacher see them? **NO**

Can my coach see them? **NO**

Can my preacher see them? **NO**

Can my principal see them? **NO**

Can my friend's parents see them? **NO**

Can my neighbor see them? **NO**

Can my friends touch them? **NO**

Can my uncle or aunt touch them? **NO**

Can my sister or brother touch them? **NO**

Can my cousin touch them? **NO**

Can my teacher touch them? **NO**

Can my coach touch them? **NO**

Can my preacher touch them? **NO**

Can my principal touch them? **NO**

Can my friend's parents touch them? **NO**

Can my neighbor touch them? **NO**

Keep your private parts private.

Do **NOT** let people see or touch them.

Other people should keep their private parts private.

They should **NOT** ask you to look at them or touch them.

If anyone asks to see or

touch your private

parts, say

NO!

Then tell a grownup.

If anyone asks you to

look at or touch their

private parts, say

NO!

Then tell a grownup.

If anyone has ever touched your private parts tell a grownup **NOW**!

If anyone has ever made you touch their private parts, tell a grownup right **NOW**!

NEVER keep these things a secret!

IF YOU BELIEVE A CHILD HAS BEEN HARMED, REPORT IT.

- *VISIT RAINN'S STATE LAW DATABASE TO SEE WHERE TO REPORT TO IN YOUR STATE.*

- *TEXT OR CALL THE CHILDHELP NATIONAL ABUSE HOTLINE AT 1-800-422-4453 TO BE CONNECTED WITH A TRAINED VOLUNTEER.*

If you would like to speak with someone who is trained to help, call the National Sexual Assault Hotline at 800.656.HOPE (4673).

You can also chat with them online at online.rainn.org

Made in the USA
Coppell, TX
28 November 2020